KU-527-331

Dirty Bertie

PONG!

DAVID ROBERTS WRITTEN BY ALAN MACDONALD

Collect all the
Dirty Bertie books!

WITHDRAWN FROM STOCK

3 0012 00130254 5

Dirty Bertie

PONG!

WITHDRAWN FROM STOCK

For Thomas Truong ~ D R
For Harry, Jack and Alfie – with whiffy wishes
~ A M

STRIPES PUBLISHING
An imprint of Little Tiger Press
1 The Coda Centre, 189 Munster Road,
London SW6 6AW

A paperback original
First published in Great Britain in 2012

Characters created by David Roberts
Text copyright © Alan MacDonald, 2012
Illustrations copyright © David Roberts, 2012

ISBN: 978-1-84715-226-8

The right of Alan MacDonald and David Roberts to
be identified as the author and illustrator of this work
respectively has been asserted by them in accordance
with the Copyright, Designs and Patents Act, 1988.

All rights reserved.

A CIP catalogue record for this book is available from
the British Library.

This book is sold subject to the condition that it shall not,
by way of trade or otherwise, be lent, resold, hired out, or
otherwise circulated without the publisher's prior consent
in any form of binding or cover other than that in which it
is published and without a similar condition, including this
condition, being imposed upon the subsequent purchaser.

Printed and bound in the UK.

10 9 8 7 6 5 4 3

Contents

CHAPTER 1

It was Friday night and Bertie's family were eating supper. Bertie loved Friday nights. The whole weekend lay ahead with nothing to spoil it.

"UGH! What's that terrible smell?" said Dad, wrinkling his nose.

Everyone looked at Bertie. "What? It wasn't me!" said Bertie. "It was Suzy!"

Dirty Bertie

"IT WAS NOT!" cried Suzy, turning pink.

"Well, *something* smells," said Dad, getting up from the table.

Mum sniffed the air. "Pooh! I can smell it too!"

Bertie went on eating his chips. What a lot of fuss over a little pong! Anyone would have thought he'd dropped a stink bomb or something.

Dad was hunting round the room, sniffing like a bloodhound. Suddenly he stopped and pulled a face.

"UGH! IT'S WHIFFER!"

Whiffer looked up from his cushion and lazily scratched his ear.

"EWW! He pongs! He reeks!" cried Suzy, holding her nose.

"Bertie, you'll have to see to him," said Mum.

"ME?" said Bertie. "Why me?"

"Because he's *your* dog!"

"But I can't help it if he smells a bit," said Bertie. "Dogs are meant to smell."

"Not like that," said Dad. "It's put me right off my dinner."

"What's he been doing?" demanded Mum.

"Nothing!" said Bertie. "I just took him to the park for a walk."

This was partly true. Whiffer had zoomed around the park chasing birds and squirrels as usual. It was on the way home that things had started to get messy. They had passed the big cow-field

and Whiffer had got overexcited. He'd
squeezed through a hole under the
fence, forcing Bertie to let go of his lead.
Luckily, there were no cows, only a lot of
cowpats. But Whiffer had raced around
and come out ponging to high heaven.

"Well, whatever he's been doing, he needs a bath," said Mum.

BATH? Whiffer pricked up his ears.

"But why do I have to do it?" grumbled Bertie.

"Because you won't get any pocket money until you do," said Dad.

Bertie's shoulders sagged. So much for a perfect weekend! Getting Whiffer to take a bath was impossible. He HATED baths! All that rubbing and scrubbing in soapy water! Bertie knew just how he felt. If he had his way, bath-time would be against the law.

"You can do it in the garden," said Mum.

"What's wrong with the bathroom?" asked Bertie.

"Oh no!" said Mum grimly. "Not after last time."

Dirty Bertie

Bertie remembered. Last time the bathroom had got a teeny bit messy. He sighed and got down from the table.

"Whiffer! Come on, boy!"

But Whiffer had disappeared. At the mention of the word "bath" he'd slipped upstairs to hide.

CHAPTER 2

Half an hour later, Bertie stood in the front garden, armed with a sponge and a bottle of Paddypaws Dog Shampoo. He wore a waterproof anorak, washing-up gloves and welly boots. When you were bathing Whiffer it was best to be prepared. A plastic bath of soapy water sat on the lawn untouched.

Dirty Bertie

Whiffer was hiding in the bushes, refusing to come out. Bertie had already chased him round the back garden and in and out of the shed. But finally he had him cornered. The front gate was shut and there was no escape.

"Whiffer! Here, boy!" he called, whistling.

Whiffer didn't budge. Bertie dug in his pocket and pulled out his secret weapon – a crunchy dog biscuit.

"Oh, Whiffer! Look what I've got!" Whiffer's head peeped out above the bush. He loved dog biscuits, especially the crunchy ones. He slunk forward, wagging his tail.

"What's this, eh?" cooed Bertie.

14

Dirty Bertie

Whiffer hung back. He could see the soapy water and he knew what that meant. On the other hand, he wanted that dog biscuit. He crept closer, his tongue hanging out. Bertie waited till he was in arm's reach.

"GOTCHA!" he cried, grabbing him by the collar.

"WOOF!" yelped Whiffer, trying to escape. Bertie pulled. Whiffer pulled back. One more heave and...

"ARGHHH!" SPLASH!

Bertie lost his grip and tumbled backwards.

Dirty Bertie

"HA HA HA!" jeered a voice. "Having a nice bath, Bertie?"

Bertie wiped his eyes and looked up at a goofy face peering over the wall. It was Royston Rich, the biggest show-off in the school. He had a snooty-nosed dog with him that was as tall as he was.

"What do you want?" scowled Bertie.

"I was just passing," said Royston. "This is Duke, by the way. He's a pedigree Great Dane."

Whiffer trotted over to get a closer look at the newcomer. He growled.

"My dad says pedigree dogs are the best," Royston boasted. "Duke's won hundreds of prizes. I'm entering him in the Pudsley Dog Show."

"Bully for you," yawned Bertie.

"You're just jealous 'cos your dog would come last," sneered Royston. "My dad says to keep Duke away from mongrels."

"Huh, Whiffer's cleverer than your dog," said Bertie.

"Oh yeah?" said Royston. "Duke can do tricks. Give me a dog biscuit."

Bertie reluctantly handed one over.

"Sit, Duke!" said Royston. Duke sat. Royston balanced the biscuit on the dog's nose. Duke didn't move. Whiffer's tongue was hanging out.

"Wait, wait…" said Royston sternly.

"One, two, three … HUP!"

Duke flicked his head, catapulting the biscuit into the air. Suddenly, he leaped high, catching the treat in his mouth.

SNAP!

Whiffer whined pitifully.

"There!" crowed Royston. "What do you think of that?"

Bertie shrugged. "Any dog could do it."

"Yours couldn't!" jeered Royston.

18

Dirty Bertie

"My dad says Duke's going to win Best in Show – that's the top prize."

"Huh!" scoffed Bertie. "I bet Whiffer could beat him."

Royston stuck out his goofy teeth. "Then why don't you enter him, smarty pants?"

"Who says I won't?" said Bertie.

"Good," said Royston. "See you on Sunday. Your dog will come last. Ha ha!"

Bertie watched as Royston flounced off with Duke, their noses in the air. *What a show-off!* he thought. Well, he would teach him a lesson. How hard could it be to win a dog show? Wait a minute though, did Royston say Sunday? *This* Sunday? That meant he only had one day to turn Whiffer into a prize-winning pooch!

CHAPTER 3

Sunday morning came, but Whiffer still hadn't had a bath. Mum was losing patience. She said the stink was so bad she'd had to spray every room with air freshener. Desperate measures were needed – especially as the dog show was due to start at three o'clock. Bertie filled the bath to the brim and emptied

Dirty Bertie

in a bottle of bubble bath. He hurried
downstairs, laying a trail of dog biscuits
as he went. All he had to do now was
hide in the bathroom and wait.

CRUNCH! CRUNCH!

His plan was working! Whiffer plodded
up the stairs, stopping to munch the
biscuits. A moment later, his head poked
round the door. The final dog biscuit was
lying on the bath mat.

"YAAAARGH!" Bertie sprang from
behind the door.

"WOOF!" barked Whiffer, as the two of them wrestled and fell backwards…

"ARGHH!" SPLASH!

Downstairs in the kitchen, Mum had just sat down with a cup of coffee.

PLOP! A drip of water landed on the table. She frowned and looked up.

PLOP!

A second drip hit her in the eye. What on earth…? Water was dripping from the ceiling!

She rushed upstairs to the bathroom. "BERTIE – ARE YOU … ARGHH!"

She skidded and went flying. There was water everywhere – on the floor and pouring over the bath! Bertie and Whiffer wrestled and fought in a mountain of bubbles.

Mum scrambled to her feet.

"BERTIE!" she screamed. "LOOK
WHAT YOU'VE DONE!"

Bertie looked around. He gulped.
The floor had got a tiny bit wet. Muddy
towels lay in a soggy heap. Bubbles
trickled over the side of the bath and
floated round the toilet.

"Well, what have you got to say?"
demanded Mum.

"Ooops!" said Bertie.

Dirty Bertie

At half-past two, Bertie set off for
Pudsley Hall. It had taken ages to mop
up the bathroom floor. But at least
Whiffer was clean. His coat was brushed
and smelled sweetly of shampoo. Bertie
thought he ought to at least win the
Best Kept Dog prize. But as long as he
beat Royston and his snooty pooch he
didn't care. Whiffer tugged at his lead.
Uh oh, Bertie had forgotten they'd have
to pass the cow-field. Cow-fields meant
cowpats…

WOOF!

Whiffer was off, streaking towards the
hole under the fence as Bertie tried to
hang on.

"WHIFFER, NO! WAIT!"

CHAPTER 4

Twenty minutes later, Bertie arrived at the hall, hot and out of breath. The dog show had already started. Dogs of all kinds were parading round a ring with their owners. Bertie spotted Duke trotting beside Royston like a show pony. A woman in a big hat was inspecting the dogs as they went past.

Dirty Bertie

Bertie tapped her on the arm.

"Scuse me…"

The woman turned around. Help, it was Miss Bowser! Bertie hadn't forgotten Whiffer's dog-training classes last year. From the look on her face Miss Bowser hadn't forgotten them either.

"YOU!" she glared. "What are you doing here?"

"I'm … um … here for the dog show," said Bertie.

Miss Bowser pointed to rows of seats. "Spectators over there," she snapped.

"I haven't come to watch," said Bertie. "Whiffer's in the show."

Miss Bowser turned pale. "Very well," she sighed. "Hurry up and join the

Dirty Bertie

others. And I'm warning you, keep that
dog under control!"

Bertie and Whiffer joined the others
parading round the ring. After five
minutes Miss Bowser told everyone to
form a line with their dogs. Bertie stood
on the end next to Royston, who
wrinkled his nose.

"What's that horrible stink?" he said.

"Dunno. Must be you," replied Bertie.

Miss Bowser came along the line. She stopped at Duke and admired his glossy coat.

"Splendid!" she said. "First class!"

Royston shot Bertie a smug look. Next she came to Whiffer.

"What IS that awful smell?"

Bertie looked around. "I can't smell anything," he said.

"It's horrible," said Miss Bowser. "It smells like … like…"

The other dog owners could smell it too. They held their noses. The dogs pulled at their leads, wanting to sniff round Whiffer. Miss Bowser took out a hanky.

"Really!" she said. "It's disgusting! Where's it coming from?"

Dirty Bertie

Royston raised his hand. "Please, Miss Bowser," he said. "I think it's Bertie's dog."

Miss Bowser bent down. She sniffed.

"UGH!" she cried. "This dog has trodden in something!"

"It's only cow poo," said Bertie.

"WHAT?"

"I got most of it off. Look – I used my hanky!"

Bertie produced a filthy brown tissue. Miss Bowser drew back as if it was the Black Death.

Dirty Bertie

"Get away, you horrible child!" she snapped. "You are disqualified! Take your filthy dog and go!"

Bertie trudged from the ring in disgrace. It wasn't fair. After all the trouble he'd been through getting Whiffer in the bath! It was all Royston's fault. He'd get that sneaky telltale.

Bertie sat in the front row, watching gloomily. For some reason no one wanted to sit next to him and Whiffer. The dog show dragged on and on, but at last there were only three dogs left. A poodle, a bulldog and Duke – all up for the title of Best in Show.

Bertie sighed. *No prizes for guessing who'll win*, he thought. Royston would

be boasting about it for the next
hundred years.

Whiffer was growing tired of sitting
still. Bertie felt in his pocket. He only had
one dog biscuit left. But maybe Whiffer
ought to earn it? He sat him down, then
placed the biscuit carefully on his nose.
Whiffer went cross-
eyed looking at it.

"Wait," said Bertie
sternly. "Wait… One,
two, three … HUP!"

Whiffer jerked back
his head. The dog biscuit spun high
in the air. Up it went, landing with a
soft plop in the ring. *Uh oh*, thought
Bertie. The next moment, Whiffer had
leaped over the barrier after the biscuit,
barking excitedly.

Dirty Bertie

WOOF! WOOF! WOOF!

Three dogs turned their heads. Duke had seen Whiffer and what's more he'd spotted the dog biscuit. He growled. Whiffer stood over his prize, bristling.

"HEEL, BOY!" yelled Royston. But it was no use. Duke took off like a hurricane on four legs. The poodle and the bulldog gave chase. In no time,

there was a scrum of snarling, yapping dogs, fighting over one biscuit. Miss Bowser had gone purple with rage. She saw Bertie climb over the barrier.

"YOU!" she thundered. "THIS IS YOUR DOING! WAIT TILL I GET MY HANDS ON YOU!"

"Crumbs!" gasped Bertie. It was time to make a quick exit.

Dirty Bertie

At five o'clock the front door slammed.
Bertie was back with Whiffer.

"Well, how did it go?" asked Mum.

"Oh … I … um, didn't stay till the end,"
said Bertie. "It was getting a bit boring."

"I can imagine," said Mum. "All those
dogs showing off! So Whiffer didn't get
into the final?"

"Not exactly," said Bertie. "I don't think
he's that keen on dog shows."

"No," said Mum. "I don't expect
they're very keen on him either."

She watched Whiffer trot past her,
heading for his dog bowl. As usual he'd
trailed muddy paw prints all through the
kitchen. She sniffed. Wait a minute…
WHAT WAS THAT TERRIBLE SMELL?

Dirty Bertie

CHAPTER 1

Bertie sat at the back of the coach as it set off. At last they were on their way! Four whole days at Barnswood Outdoor Centre! At Barnswood they had climbing walls, rope walks, go-karts, even archery. And best of all, Bertie would be sharing a room with Darren and Eugene. They could stay up late having midnight feasts

without boring parents telling them to
go to bed.

"Quiet! Everyone look this way!"

Bertie groaned. He'd forgotten Miss
Boot was coming too. School trips
would be so much more fun if they left
the teachers behind.

Miss Boot stood at the front of the
coach holding a clipboard. "Pay
attention," she barked. "I am going to
read out the room list so everyone
knows where they are sleeping."

Bertie leaned forward eagerly. He
hoped it was just the three of them —
they didn't want to share with anyone
who actually wanted to sleep.

"Sophie, Donna, Lucy…" Miss Boot
droned on, checking off the names. Finally
she reached the ones that mattered.

"Room Seven: Darren, Eugene … and Nicholas."

"WHAT?" cried Know-All Nick.

"WHAT?" gasped Bertie. He wasn't sharing with his friends?

"But what about me?" he cried.

"I am coming to you," said Miss Boot grimly. "Room Ten: Trevor, Warren … and Bertie. That's everyone. Please remember your room number. I won't be telling you again." She sat down.

Bertie sank slowly in his seat. This was a disaster!

"She's split us up!" he moaned.

"I know!" said Eugene glumly. "I can't believe it."

"And we've got Know-All Nick," grumbled Darren.

"At least you two are together," said Bertie. "What about me? I'm with Trevor and Warren. It'll be torture!"

"Perhaps it's a mistake," said Eugene.

"Yeah," said Darren. "Go and ask her, Bertie."

"Me?" said Bertie. "Why don't you go and ask her?"

"I'm not the one who's in the wrong room," said Darren.

Bertie hesitated. Miss Boot didn't like children bothering her with silly questions.

Then again, if he didn't do something
he'd be stuck with Trevor and Warren.
He'd rather share a room with Count
Dracula.

He made his way down to the front
where Miss Boot was sitting with Miss
Darling.

"Um, Miss?" he said.

Miss Boot looked up. "What are you
doing out of your seat? Go and sit down!"

"But Miss, it's important," said Bertie. "It's about the rooms."

Miss Boot groaned. "What about them?"

"Well, I asked to be with Darren and Eugene," explained Bertie. "They were my first choice."

"We can't all have our first choice," said Miss Boot.

"Yes, but I'm not with either of them," said Bertie. "You put me with Warren and Trevor. There must be a mistake."

Miss Boot shook her head. "I have split you up because you are always in trouble, Bertie. Especially when you're with your friends. Now you will sleep where you're told, is that clear?"

"But Miss, we won't cause any trouble," argued Bertie.

Dirty Bertie

"I said no!" snapped Miss Boot. "Now go and sit down. And Bertie – my room is right opposite yours, so I shall be keeping an eye on you."

Bertie drooped back to his seat. It was so unfair! What was the point of going on a school trip if you weren't allowed to enjoy yourself?

CHAPTER 2

Finally they arrived at Barnswood. Bertie
didn't have time to think about rooms
because there was far too much going
on. After lunch they had a go on the rope
walk, then tackled the climbing wall. Bertie
was the first to get right to the top.
Know-All Nick got halfway up, then came
over all dizzy and had to be rescued.

Miss Boot did not try the climbing wall. She claimed she wasn't wearing the right shoes.

It wasn't until after supper that Bertie remembered which room he was in. Miss Boot announced they should all get an early night as they had a busy day tomorrow. Bertie looked around as everyone trooped off to bed. Who would notice if he sneaked off to Darren and Eugene's room for a while? He put up his hood and followed his friends out of the dining hall.

"Goodnight, children!" sang Miss Darling.

"Goodnight, Miss Darling!" chorused the class.

"Night!" mumbled Bertie, as he hurried past.

"BERTIE!" roared Miss Boot. "WHERE DO YOU THINK YOU'RE GOING?"

"Um, to my room," said Bertie.

"Your room is *that* way," said Miss Boot, pointing. "And remember, I am in the room opposite. If I catch you out of bed there'll be trouble!"

One hour later, Bertie lay on the top bunk staring at the ceiling. He wasn't tired. After all, it was only ten o'clock. How was he meant to go to sleep this early? If Darren and Eugene were here they'd all be telling jokes and scoffing crisps. He poked his head over the bunk.

"Psssst! Anyone awake?"

No answer.

"Trevor!"

"What is it?" groaned Trevor.

"I'm hungry!" said Bertie.

Trevor sighed. "Go to sleep!"

"I can't, I'm starving. I only had six slices of pizza."

Trevor rolled over and pretended to sleep. Warren sniffled in the other bed.

"I know," said Bertie. "Let's raid the kitchen!"

"Nooo!" bleated Trevor.

"Why not?"

"We'll get in trouble!"

"Not if we don't get caught," said Bertie.

"Miss Boot said we have to go to sleep," said Trevor.

Bertie sighed. Trevor was about as much fun as a flat tyre. And Warren was even worse; why couldn't he stop sniffling?

"What's the matter with you?" asked
Bertie.

"I … I don't like it here!" sobbed
Warren.

"Why not?"

"I WANT MY TEDDY!" wailed
Warren. "I WANT TO GO HOME!"

Bertie rolled his eyes. This was the
worst night ever. He bet Darren and
Eugene were having loads of fun.

Along the corridor, Nick's room-mates
were keeping him awake.

"I know! Let's play the dare game!"
said Darren.

"NOO!" groaned Nick. "Miss Boot said
we have to go to sleep."

"Don't be a wimp," said Darren.
"Who's going first?"

"Nickerless!" cried Eugene.

Dirty Bertie

"Stop calling me that!" moaned Nick.

"I've got one," said Darren. "I dare you to knock on Miss Boot's door and run away."

Nick turned pale. "No way!"

"Go on, scaredy-cat," said Darren.

"You can't make me," whined Nick. "I'm not playing. I'm going to sleep!"

"Okay." Darren smiled to himself. "Let's *all* go to sleep."

There was a short silence.

"SNORK!"

Darren snored like a pig. Eugene burst out laughing. Nick hid his head under his pillow. Three nights of this was more than he could bear.

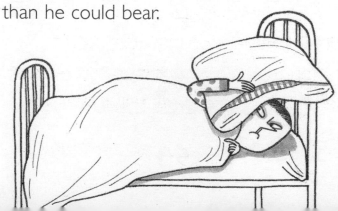

CHAPTER 3

Next morning, Bertie joined Darren and Eugene at breakfast.

"So how was last night?" asked Eugene.

Bertie groaned. "Terrible!"

"Same here," nodded Darren. "Know-All Nick never stops moaning."

"You should try being in my room," said Bertie. "Warren cries himself to sleep."

Dirty Bertie

"That's nothing. Nick tried to make us tidy our room," said Eugene.

Bertie shook his head. This was ridiculous. He hated the room he was in and so did Nick. If only they could swap places they'd both be happy. He glanced over. Nick was sitting by himself, sulking.

"Hey, Nick," said Bertie, sliding into the seat next to him.

Nick scowled. "What do you want?"

"I just wondered how you're getting on with your room-mates?"

Dirty Bertie

Nick toyed with his cereal. "They're idiots," he said. "They kept me awake all night."

Bertie nodded. "I expect you'd rather be with Trevor and Warren."

"At least they wouldn't put crisps in my bed," grumped Nick.

Bertie tried not to laugh. "So listen," he said, "why don't you and me swap rooms?"

Nick gave him a look. "How? Miss Boot won't let us."

"But she doesn't have to know," said Bertie.

"She'll know," said Nick.

"Not if we all keep our mouths shut."

Nick shook his head. "It'll never work," he sighed. "Miss Boot will find out. She can read your mind."

Dirty Bertie

Bertie gave up. He was wasting his time. Nick never risked getting in trouble. He didn't even dare blow his nose without Miss Boot's permission. The only way he'd ever change rooms was if he sleepwalked in the night. Bertie's eyes suddenly lit up. Wait a minute – that wasn't such a bad idea!

"Well?" asked Darren, when Bertie returned. "What did he say?"

Bertie shook his head. "He's too chicken – but don't worry, I've got a brilliant idea."

It was almost midnight. The corridors were silent. In Room Seven the only sound was Know-All Nick snoring.

TAP! TAP! Someone knocked softly on the door.

Dirty Bertie

"Who is it?" whispered Eugene.

"It's me, you fool!" answered Bertie.
"Is he asleep?"

"Yes! Not so loud!"

Bertie crept in. They woke up Darren and gathered round Nick's bed.

"So how are we going to move him?" asked Darren.

"Simple. Carry him," replied Bertie.

Dirty Bertie

"Don't be stupid. He's bound to wake up," said Darren.

"No he won't," said Bertie. "Not if we carry him on his mattress. He won't feel a thing."

They squatted down and lifted the mattress off the bed. Nick was a lot heavier than Bertie had expected. He weighed a ton.

"Let's go," he grunted. "Whatever you do, don't drop him!"

Dirty Bertie

They lugged Nick out of the room.
It was a tight fit squeezing the mattress
through the door. Bertie went first,
walking backwards, while Darren and
Eugene carried the other end.

"How far is it?"
moaned Darren.

"Not far,"
said Bertie.
"Keep
moving!"
They staggered
down the gloomy
corridor, puffing and
panting. Bertie
backed into a wall.
"OWW!" he yelled.
"Sshh!" hissed
Darren.

They all froze. If Miss Boot discovered them now they were dead.

"Look where you're going!" hissed Eugene.

"I am! You try walking backwards!" replied Bertie.

When they turned the corner, the corridor became even darker – there was no light at all.

"Bertie! Which one's your room?" whispered Darren.

Bertie looked round. He blinked. In the pitch black he could hardly see the doors let alone read the numbers. Which room was his?

"Hurry up!" groaned Darren. "My arms are dropping off!"

Bertie tried to remember. Was it the door on the right or the left?

Dirty Bertie

"This one," he said, making a decision. He leaned on the door handle.

CREEEEAK!

They shuffled in carrying the mattress. Nick didn't seem half so heavy now. Bertie peered around the room. Oddly it seemed bigger than he remembered.

"Where's Nick?" gasped Eugene.

"What?" said Bertie.

"Nick. He's not there!"

They all stared at the empty mattress.

"Yikes!" said Darren. "We've lost him!"

CHAPTER 4

They found Nick lying in the corridor.
He must have slid off the mattress when
Bertie leaned over to open the door.
By a miracle he was still snoring like
a baby. They heaved him on to the
mattress and got him back into the
bedroom. It was dark apart from a little
light leaking through the curtains.

Dirty Bertie

"Where do we put him?" whispered
Darren.

Bertie blinked in the darkness. Again
he had the feeling the room had grown
bigger. And where were the bunk beds?
In any case, he couldn't carry Nick any
further. They dumped him on the floor.

"Let's get out before anyone comes!"
whispered Bertie.

"Look at these!"

Eugene flapped something in his face —
a gigantic pair of pink knickers. Bertie
stared. Funny, he didn't remember Trevor
or Warren wearing pink knickers. Unless
… he swung round. On the bedside table
lay a make-up bag, some earrings and a
pair of glasses he knew all too well.

"We're in the wrong room!" he
gasped.

"What?" said Darren.

"This is Miss Boot's room!"

Sure enough there were two single beds. In one slept Miss Darling and in the other was the massive shape of Miss Boot.

Dirty Bertie

"What shall we do?" squeaked Eugene.

There was only one thing *to* do.

"RUN!" cried Bertie.

They rushed for the door. In their panic Darren stepped on something.

"ARRRRGHHH!" Know-All Nick woke up with a yell.

The noise woke the two teachers. Miss Boot shot upright in bed. She fumbled for her glasses.

"WHO'S THERE?" she bellowed.

But Bertie and his friends didn't wait to explain. They bolted out of the door and raced down the corridor back to their rooms.

Miss Boot finally found the light. CLICK!

"HELP!" screamed Miss Darling. "WHAT'S THAT?"

Dirty Bertie

On the floor was a mattress with a small lump trembling under a duvet. Miss Boot grabbed the duvet and pulled it off. Know-All Nick stared back at her in bug-eyed terror.

"IT WASN'T ME!" he wailed.

Dirty Bertie

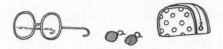

The next morning, Bertie was summoned to see Miss Boot at breakfast. She wasn't in a good mood.

"Where were you last night?" she snapped.

"Me?" said Bertie innocently. "I was in bed."

"The whole time?"

"Yes."

"You didn't leave your room?"

"No," said Bertie. "I was really sleepy. Did I miss anything?"

Miss Boot searched his face to see if he could be lying.

"I found Nicholas in my room," she said.

"*Really?*" said Bertie. "Nicholas?"

"Yes, he claims he has no idea how he got there."

Bertie shook his head. "That's weird!"

Miss Boot narrowed her eyes.

"I suppose you don't know anything about it?" she said.

Bertie shook his head. "Maybe he sleepwalks?"

"Hmm," said Miss Boot. She sighed wearily. "Anyway, I need to keep an eye on Nicholas, so I'm moving him in with Warren and Trevor."

"Oh?" said Bertie.

"Yes, you will have to move out," said Miss Boot. "There's a bed in Darren and Eugene's room. I'm sure you don't mind?"

"Mind?" said Bertie. "Um, no, not at all."

"Good. That's settled then," said Miss Boot. "Off you go."

Dirty Bertie

Bertie scarpered before Miss Boot had second thoughts.

Darren and Eugene were waiting for him anxiously.

"Well?" asked Darren. "What did she say?"

Bertie gave them a big thumbs up.

"Midnight feasts here we come!"

CHAPTER 1

It was lunchtime. Bertie and his friends zoomed across the playground. Bertie was Rocketman swooping out of the sky.

"NEEEEEEOWWWWW!"

He whizzed past Miss Skinner and Miss Boot and jumped on Know-All Nick.

"Thought you could escape, eh?"

Dirty Bertie

"MISS!" wailed Nick. "Bertie's being mean!"

"Bertie!" yelled Miss Boot. "Stop that!"

"And do up your shoelaces!" cried Miss Skinner. She sighed heavily. "Sometimes I despair of the children in this school. Just look at that boy."

Bertie was bending down to do up his shoelaces. His jumper was on back to front, his shirt was hanging out and his jeans were filthy.

"He always looks like that," said Miss Boot.

"That's my point," said the head teacher. "He's a disgrace. What would people think if they saw him now? They'd wonder what kind of school he went to."

Miss Boot rolled her eyes. She could tell Miss Skinner was warming up for one of her pep talks. Any minute now she would start on about Swotter House.

"I mean look at Swotter House," said Miss Skinner. "Have you seen the children at that school?"

Miss Boot nodded. The bus for Swotter House stopped on her road. Every morning, she watched the children get on quietly without pushing or shoving. They all looked impossibly neat – as if they'd just been ironed.

Dirty Bertie

"Those children are a credit to their school," Miss Skinner went on. "Smart blazers, neat ties, grey socks. Why can't Bertie look like that?"

Miss Boot could think of a thousand reasons. Bertie was probably the grubbiest boy ever born. Despite his parents' best efforts, he always arrived looking like a scarecrow. As for what he kept in his pockets … Miss Boot shuddered to think!

"Bertie!" called Miss Skinner, beckoning him over.

"I wasn't doing anything," protested Bertie.

"I just want to ask you something," said Miss Skinner. "How would you like to look smart?"

Bertie pulled a face. "What for?"

"Well, because everyone likes to look smart," said Miss Skinner.

"I don't," said Bertie.

"Yes, but you should," said Miss Skinner. "For instance, what if you had a splendid new uniform?"

Bertie frowned. "I wouldn't mind a fireman's uniform," he said, "with big boots and a helmet."

"I was talking about a school uniform," said Miss Skinner.

"Oh," said Bertie flatly. "You mean like ties and stuff?"

"Yes, exactly," said Miss Skinner.

Bertie wiped his nose on the back of his hand. "No thanks," he said. "I'm okay as I am. Um, can I go now?"

73

Dirty Bertie

"Very well," sighed Miss Skinner.

They watched Bertie run off and throw himself on Darren. The two of them rolled around in the dirt.

"You see," said the head. "That's what we're up against. What we need is more children like Nicholas."

They glanced at Know-All Nick, who was using his hanky to wipe a speck of dust off his shoe.

"The answer is obvious," said Miss Skinner. "We need a school uniform."

Miss Boot looked at her. "Uniform?

You're not serious?"

"Perfectly," said Miss Skinner. "Children would take pride in a uniform. We wouldn't have buttons missing or socks drooping round ankles."

"But we've never had a uniform," said Miss Boot.

"Then it's high time we started," replied Miss Skinner.

Miss Boot rubbed her chin. School uniform ... maybe it would work? But Bertie in school uniform — that was another matter.

CHAPTER 2

The following week, Bertie brought a letter home from school. Mum found it screwed up in his coat pocket.

"What's this?" she said, holding up a dog-eared piece of paper.

"Oh yeah," said Bertie. "I was going to give it to you. It's just some stuff about school."

Mum shook her head. She doubted if half the letters from school ever made it home. She unfolded the letter and started to read.

"School uniform?" she said. "Goodness!"

"I know," groaned Bertie. "Miss Skinner's gone bonkers."

"Actually, I think it's a very good idea," said Mum.

"Why?" asked Bertie. "What's the point!"

"Well, because it looks smart," said Mum.

Bertie blew out his cheeks. "People keep saying that, but I don't want to look smart! What's wrong with the way I am?"

Mum gave him a withering look.

"I like dressing like this," moaned Bertie.

"Why do I need a smelly old uniform?"

"So you can be proud of your school,"
said Mum. "It shows you go to Pudsley
Junior."

"I already know that!" said Bertie.
"I don't need a uniform to remind me!"

Mum turned over the letter and read
the back. There was another surprise at
the end. Miss Skinner was launching a
competition.

"What a lovely idea!" cried Mum.
"Miss Skinner wants you all to think of
a design for the new uniform. Just think,
Bertie, it could be your idea that's
chosen."

"I know," said Bertie.

"Well, don't you think that's exciting?"
Bertie shrugged. "It will be if I win."

Miss Skinner had given the idea a lot

of thought. She wanted the whole
school to be as excited about the new
uniform as she was. And the best way to
achieve that was through a competition.
No one could resist a competition – not
even Bertie.

"You'd better get thinking," said Mum.
"Have you got any ideas?"

"Millions," said Bertie. The problem
was choosing just one.

Dirty Bertie

After supper, he sat down with pencil and paper and a supply of biscuits. At the top of the page he wrote SKOOL UNIFORM. Then he ate a biscuit. He wrote TIE, BLAZER, SHIRT – then crossed them all out. What was the point of a uniform that would be like all the others? What his school needed was something new. Something that would make other schools turn green with envy.

Bertie chewed the end of his pencil. Astronauts had good uniforms, so did pirate captains. He wouldn't mind dressing as a pirate to go to school. Better still, what about SUPERHEROES? Bertie had always wanted to be a superhero. Imagine zooming through the sky! Bertie began drawing a few ideas. Ten minutes later he had his design.

It was brilliant! Smart, clever, useful —
the school uniform of the future.
What's more, it was bound to win the
competition. Wait till Miss Skinner saw it
— she would be astonished!

CHAPTER 3

A week later, Bertie sat in assembly
with Darren and Eugene. Today was
the big day. All the entries were in and
Miss Skinner was going to announce
the winner of the competition. Bertie
could hardly sit still. He had seen some
of the other entries and they were
all rubbish.

Dirty Bertie

Eugene had drawn a boring
old sweatshirt with the school
badge on the front. Darren's
idea was a black
hoodie bearing
the skull and
crossbones.
Angela Nicely
wanted pink
cardigans with
rows of fluffy bunnies. Bertie's
design was a million times better
than any of them. After all, who
didn't want to dress like a superhero?

DARREN

Eugene

angela

Miss Skinner swept into the hall carrying
a large envelope.

"Good morning, children," she said.
"As you all know, today we will find out
the winner of our Design a Uniform

Competition. We have had hundreds of super entries, but we can only choose one winner. I'm sure you're all dying to know who that is."

She gazed at the rows of eager faces. Everyone held their breath. Bertie got ready to jump up when his name was called. He watched Miss Skinner take the piece of paper from the envelope. He leaned forward. *This is it! he* thought.

"And the winner is…" Miss Skinner looked up and smiled. "Nicholas!"

Bertie gasped. Know-All Nick? What a fix! How could that frog-faced sneak have won?

Everyone clapped politely. Nick made his way to the front and shook Miss Skinner's hand. He spotted Bertie's scowling face and gave him a sickly smile.

Dirty Bertie

"Well done, Nicholas," beamed Miss Skinner. "We all agreed that your design was marvellous. Simple, strong and very smart. Perhaps you'd like to show it to the whole school?"

Nick took his design and held it up for all to see. Bertie's jaw dropped. You had to be kidding.

"YUCK!" he cried. It came out louder than he'd intended.

Miss Skinner glared. "Who said that?"

"It was Bertie, Miss," smirked Nick.

"Bertie, I will not have rudeness in assembly!" snapped Miss Skinner. "Come and see me at break time."

Bertie's shoulders drooped. He had only said what everyone was thinking. Nick's design was horrible. Yellow and green stripes? It looked like someone had been sick on it.

After assembly they all trooped back to their class.

"Trust Know-All Nick to win," groaned Darren.

"Yeah, what a creep!" said Eugene. "Just cos his mum's a school governor!"

Bertie stuffed his hands in his pockets.

Dirty Bertie

"You know what this means?" he said.
"We'll all have to wear that stupid
stripey blazer."

"And a tie," said Eugene.

"And a cap!" added
Darren in disgust.
They walked
in gloomy
silence.

"Well, I'm
not putting up with
it," said Bertie. "You won't
catch me in a cap."

"What are you going to do?" asked
Eugene.

"I don't know yet," said Bertie. "But I'll
think of something."

Dirty Bertie

At break, Bertie reported to Miss Skinner's office, but when he knocked, there was no answer. He peeped round the door. The head wasn't there. Bertie stood for a moment wondering what to do. He sat down in Miss Skinner's swivel chair and whizzed around a few times. CRASH! A pile of books fell on the floor. Bertie jumped off the chair and rushed to pick them up. Wait a minute – what was this? A letter on the desk addressed to Dapper's Schoolwear. The envelope hadn't been sealed. Bertie checked the coast was clear, then carefully took out the letter.

Dear Sir, 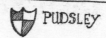 PUDSLEY

I am delighted to send you the design for our new school uniform. The idea came from one of our brightest children. I'm sure you'll agree it is going to look wonderful. As we discussed, we will need the first order of 200 uniforms in time for next term.

Yours impatiently,

Miss D. Skinner, Head teacher

Nick's winning design was clipped to the back. Bertie stared at it in disgust. No way was he wearing those terrible trousers! That dopey blazer! That stupid cap! But wait – maybe he didn't have to… He smiled to himself as he selected one of Miss Skinner's red pens. Now to add a few little ideas of his own…

CHAPTER 4

A few weeks later, Miss Skinner came into assembly carrying a large parcel. "Can anyone guess what's in here?" she asked.

Darren raised his hand. "A big bar of chocolate!"

"No, far more exciting than that," cried Miss Skinner. "It's our new school uniform! The very first one!"

"Hooray!" cried Know-All Nick. Darren and Eugene rolled their eyes.

"Nicholas," beamed Miss Skinner. "As this is your design you should be the first to try it on."

Nick pushed his way up to the stage, bursting with pride.

Bertie leaned over to Darren and whispered, "This should be worth watching."

Nick tore open the parcel to reveal a box, and hurried behind the curtain to get changed. He pulled out a pair of grey socks and put them on. Next came a stripey tie. He knotted it and reached into the box. The colour drained from his face.

"Hurry up!" called Miss Skinner. "We're dying to see!"

Nick gulped.

He put on the cap – it had sprouted a pair of silver wings. He tried on the blazer. It had a silver cape that hung to the floor. There were sparkly boots instead of shoes, and the trousers were silver and skintight.

"Come along now!" cried Miss Skinner.

Know-All Nick stepped out from

Dirty Bertie

behind the curtain.

Miss Skinner gaped. Miss Boot looked like she might explode. Children were starting to giggle. The giggles grew louder and became hoots of laughter.

"HEE HEE! HOO HOO! HA HA!"

Know-All Nick had turned bright pink. What had happened to his beautiful design? Who could have done this?

Seated in the front row, Bertie was
feeling pretty pleased with himself. All in
all he thought the uniform looked pretty
good. And with the rocket boots, Nick
could zoom into outer space and never
come back…

Darren and Eugene were both staring
at him in awe.

"Okay," said Darren at last. "I give in.
How did you do it?"

Bertie shrugged. "I just added a few
ideas of my own." Suddenly, a thought
struck him. "Hey, I wonder how many
uniforms Miss Skinner has ordered?"

Eugene gasped. "Probably hundreds!"

Bertie's eyes shone. He couldn't wait
for next term! It was going to be
super-tastic!

Out now: